THE WAY

"Mark was a starter before Jo joined the team," Brian said. "Now he never gets to start anymore."

"And don't forget about Chunky and MJ," Dave added. "There are some games they barely get in at all. That must not feel too cool."

"Easy for you to say," Will retorted. "You're not being benched so they can play."

"I'm not saying I *agree* with what Jim and Nate are doing," Dave said. "I'm just saying I kind of get what they're thinking."

"I get what they're thinking too," Will answered hotly. "It's just that everyone around here is doing too *much* thinking. We should be trying to win basketball games. Whatever it takes—*whoever* it takes—that's the way we have to go."

Don't miss any of the books in

super HOOPS

—a slammin', jammin', in-your-face action series
from Bantam Books!

WHO'S THE MAN?

by
Hank Herman

BANTAM BOOKS
NEW YORK · TORONTO · LONDON · SYDNEY · AUCKLAND

RL 2.6, 007-010

WHO'S THE MAN?

A Bantam Book / November 1997

Produced by Daniel Weiss Associates, Inc.
33 West 17th Street
New York, NY 10011.

Cover art by Jeff Mangiat.

All rights reserved.

Copyright © 1997 by Daniel Weiss Associates, Inc., and
Hank Herman.

ISBN: 0-553-48477-X
Published simultaneously in the United States and Canada

Bantam Books are published by Bantam Books, a division of Bantam
Doubleday Dell Publishing Group, Inc. Its trademark, consisting of the
words "Bantam Books" and the portrayal of a rooster, is Registered in U.S.
Patent and Trademark Office and in other countries. Marca Registrada.
Bantam Books, 1540 Broadway, New York, New York 10036.

PRINTED IN THE UNITED STATES OF AMERICA

OPM   0 9 8 7 6 5 4 3 2 1

To the Steiners, athletes all

CHAPTER 1

SCREECH!

The shrill scream of the referee's whistle filled the gym—again! Will Hopwood's fists closed in anger. It was the very sound he didn't want to hear.

Will knew that the ref had made the right call, that he *had* fouled his man. But how could you *avoid* making

1

contact with Moose Williams? Once the Lions' strong, burly center began rumbling to the hoop, it was impossible to stop him without physical force.

The personal foul was Will's third—and the second half had just begun. As he took his position along the lane, waiting for Moose's free throws, he saw Brian Simmons, his friend and teammate, shrug his shoulders in a gesture of sympathy. *What can you do?* Brian seemed to be saying.

Will also noticed his brother, Jim, conferring with Nate Bowman, the Bulls' other teenage coach, on the sideline. They both glanced down the bench in the direction of Chunky Schwartz, the whale-shaped backup center.

Obviously, the coaches were thinking, *Will's in foul trouble. Let's get him out of there and save him for crunch time.*

Will waved his arms until the coaches looked his way. "I'll be all right," he mouthed silently. "Don't worry. I won't foul out."

As well as being the coaches of the

basketball-crazy Branford Bulls, Jim and Nate were also best friends and co-captains of the Branford High varsity basketball team. Nate was the better player—probably the best high-school prospect in the county. But Jim usually made the tough coaching decisions for the fifth-grade Bulls.

Now, as the ref handed the ball to Moose, Will watched the two coaches becoming involved in what looked like a heated discussion. Nate always wanted to get all the subs in early. Jim was much more conservative—he liked to stay with the starters as long as he could.

Since Chunky wasn't sent in to replace Will, it was obvious that Jim had won the argument . . . as usual.

Will watched as Moose planted his hefty body on the foul line. Though at five-foot-two Moose was two inches shorter than Will, the bulky Plainview center outweighed him by a good twenty pounds. He had chest muscles Will had never seen before in a fifth-grader, and his blond crew cut added to his tough-guy look.

Lucky for us, Will thought, *this Incredible Hulk has a gorilla's touch on his free throws.* Will had already sent him to the line to shoot twice in the first half, and Moose was oh-for-four so far.

True to form, Moose's first shot this time around was a brick off the back

iron. To Will, the second shot looked just as ugly—but it banged off the glass backboard and fell neatly through the hoop.

Lucky stiff, Will thought.

Moose's successful free throw triggered a loud burst of thrilled—and surprised—cheering from the home fans in the Plainview YMCA gym. With the score at 24–22, the Lions were now within two points of the heavily favored Bulls.

Will wasn't all that surprised. *Why does this happen to us so often?* he asked himself angrily. *We play great against the Slashers and the Panthers, the really good teams. But when we play the weak teams, we drop right down to their level!*

Jim and Nate constantly reminded the Bulls about this unfortunate habit—and Will couldn't blame them!

As Will passed the ball to the Bulls' guard David Danzig and ran down-court, he considered the fact that opening-day jitters might have something to do with the Bulls' spotty performance. This was the first game of a new season. The Branford Bulls were always one of the top teams in the Danville County Basketball League. The Plainview Lions were usually down near the bottom. In a funny way, that put a lot of pressure on the Bulls.

"Come on, guys. Let's break it open! *Now!*" Mark Fisher bellowed urgently from the bench. Mark, the Bulls' sixth man, was the team clown—when the Bulls were on top. He was the first to panic, however, when things got tense.

But the Bulls weren't able to break the game open in the third quarter. Neither team managed to get any momentum going. They traded baskets and the Bulls hung on to their narrow lead.

With less than two minutes to go in the period, Terrell Means, the Lions' shooting guard, delivered a bounce pass to Moose Williams in the paint. As Moose turned to the hoop, Will jumped into his path and was bowled over by the barrel-chested center.

Will heard the referee's whistle. As he was pulled to his feet by team-mates Brian Simmons and Derek Roberts, Will wore a self-satisfied look on his face. He assumed he'd drawn the charge from Moose.

But instead, he saw the ref thrusting his two hands to his hips while calling out, "Number fourteen, red!"

So Moose Williams *wasn't* being called for the charge. Instead, *Will himself* had been called for a blocking foul! One more personal and he'd be out of the game!

"No way!" Will cried, running after the official. Both Jim and Nate considered Ron Sparks, the short, muscular, African American referee, to be the best official in the league. *But he sure blew this call!* Will thought.

"I had position," Will pleaded to Mr. Sparks. "He ran right over me!"

"Sorry, son," the referee answered evenly. "You were still moving your feet. You weren't set. The foul's on you."

Mr. Sparks's voice was friendly enough, but there was a firmness in the tone that said *end of discussion.*

Will still had a mouthful he was bursting to say, but he managed to hold his tongue. As Moose made his way to the line for the first of his two free throws, Will's attention was caught by activity on the Bulls' bench. Chunky had gotten up and was slowly moving in the direction of the coaches.

Chunky's right to assume he's coming in, Will thought. *This one's kind of a no-brainer. I've got four personal fouls and we're still in the third quarter. Chunky's got to come in for a while so I don't foul out.*

Will saw Jim and Nate having words. Then Nate walked away from Jim, shaking his head. Chunky returned to his seat on the bench, his head hanging dejectedly.

He's not coming in for me after all! Will realized. He was glad—but extremely surprised.

"Come on, Will!" Jim barked. "Hang

in there. Don't pick up that fifth foul!"

In a flash, Will figured out exactly what had happened. Jim was intent upon the Bulls winning their first game of the new season, and he didn't think they could do it with Chunky guarding Moose. He preferred to stick with Will, hoping that his younger brother could somehow avoid fouling out.

It was also clear to Will that Nate had strongly disagreed with Jim's decision—and that Chunky was pretty disappointed by it too.

Will felt a little bad for Chunky but not *that* bad. *First, we've got to win,* Will thought. *We can deal with people's feelings later!*

On the floor, Derek and Jo Meyerson, the starting shooting guard, were also shaking their heads. *Obviously,* Will realized, *Nate and Chunky aren't the only ones unhappy with Jim's thinking.* But the encouraging thumbs-up sign he received from Brian and the low five he got from Dave—his two best friends on the team—made it clear that at least a couple of Will's teammates agreed with Jim's decision.

Standing along the lane, Will watched as Moose missed his first free throw and made his second— same results as the center's last trip to the line.

As he jogged down to the Bulls' offensive end of the floor, Will found himself agreeing with his brother's thinking wholeheartedly.

Sending Chunky in to try to guard Moose Williams would be like giving *the game away,* he chuckled to himself.

Then his eyes settled on Mr. Sparks, the referee.

I just better not pick up that fifth foul, he thought as he took his position in the low post. He could feel his heart racing.

CHAPTER 2

For the last two minutes of the third quarter and for over four minutes of the fourth quarter, Will managed to perform the balancing act Jim had asked of him. He defended Moose well, while somehow steering clear of that fifth foul.

With 3:30 remaining in the final period, and the Bulls clinging to a 45–42 lead, Moose squared him-self for a jump shot.

Will's eyes lit

up. There was nothing he loved more than blocking shots! As soon as Moose's feet left the ground, Will leaped too.

Thwack!

Will sent the ball with satisfying force in the direction of the Lions' bench. But he realized he also had gotten a piece of Moose's hand as he swatted the shot away.

Screech!

Yup, there's the whistle. Man, Mr. Sparks was right on top of that one! Will thought bitterly.

The official scorer reminded the referee that it was the fifth foul on number 14, but Will didn't wait to be told. He was well aware that for him the game was over. He walked over to the Bulls' bench with his head down and grabbed his water bottle.

Will watched Chunky report to the scorer's table. He noticed that his backup didn't look as eager to play as he had been when he thought he was going in at the beginning of the third quarter.

Nerves, Will thought. *I'm used to crunch time. Chunky's not.*

Will sat on the bench between Jim and MJ Jordan, a substitute forward. Though his face was buried in his hands, Will peeked out just enough to watch 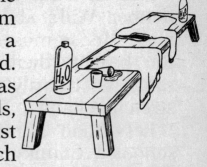 Moose shoot his free throws. His spirits lifted a bit as the wide-bodied center missed them both—by a lot!

That makes him two-for-ten from the line today, Will calculated. *Good thing Moose stinks as a free-throw shooter. If he were half decent, we'd really be up the creek!*

Unfortunately for the Bulls, however, Andy Bowers, a Plainview forward, snatched the rebound on the second brick and shoveled the ball back out to Moose.

Moose began backing in on Chunky.

"Hold your ground!" Will called. "You've got to put a body on him!"

But the Bulls' substitute center had neither Will's ability nor his toughness. Moose muscled him in close to the basket, then scored the short-range shot easily over Chunky's outstretched hands.

Less than a minute later, Moose schooled Chunky again on the same move. The Lions led, 46–45.

Will sat helplessly on the bench, growing more and more frustrated. The summer before, when Will was out of action with a broken arm, he'd helped Chunky work on his game. He'd tutored him on defense, showed him a good free-throw routine, even taught him his patented shot—the turnaround jumper.

Didn't Chunky learn anything? he found himself wondering.

With eight seconds left in the game and the Bulls down by one, Dave Danzig worked the ball in to Chunky in the paint. Chunky was well guarded by Moose Williams, and he couldn't find the open man. In desperation, he tried Will's turnaround jumper.

His shot was way off the mark, but luckily he was hammered by Moose after releasing the ball.

"Foul, number thirty-three, purple," Mr. Sparks called out. "Two shots."

From his spot on the bench, Will watched in dismay as Chunky stepped gingerly to the line. Chunky looked like he didn't want to be there in the worst way.

"I don't know why, but I'm not getting a good feeling from this," Mark said nervously. He was sitting alongside Will on the bench.

"My thoughts *exactly,*" Will agreed.

Will remembered coaching Chunky on his free-throw shooting the summer before: Bounce the ball once or twice, bend the knees, take a deep breath, let it out. Then sight the basket, let the ball roll off your fingertips with lots of rotation, and follow through.

Today, Chunky went through the entire ritual. But his shot fell short, *way* short.

Only Chunky would shoot an air ball at a time like this, Will groaned to himself. *What a choke artist!*

On his second try, Chunky, obviously fearing another air ball, shot much too hard. The ball clanged off the back iron.

Will hid his face with his hands. *I never should have fouled out!* he thought miserably. *Chunky just can't handle the pressure.*

Terrell Means grabbed the long rebound on Chunky's second miss. But the always alert Jo, her ponytail bobbing, darted over and fouled the shooting guard immediately. That stopped the clock with three seconds remaining in the game.

The Bulls were over the foul limit, so Means would be shooting one-and-one. The slim guard confidently went to the line and drained the first. With almost no hesitation, he made the second as well. Nothing but net on both shots.

The Lions led, 48–45.

The Bulls had no time-outs remaining. Jo quickly inbounded the ball to Dave under the Lions' basket. Dave dribbled three times, then took a desperation heave from half-court as the buzzer sounded. It wasn't even close.

The mighty Branford Bulls had lost the season opener to the lowly Plainview Lions.

Chunky shambled over to the Bulls' bench. His head was down, his face red.

At least he realizes his pathetic defense against Moose and his choke at the foul line cost us the game, Will thought bitterly.

Before anyone uttered a word of criticism, Chunky put up his hands and said, "You know, if I got more playing time, I wouldn't screw up in the clutch."

More playing time, Will repeated to himself. *He's always talking about more playing time. Well, if he wants more playing time, let him earn it!*

Nate placed a large, consoling hand on Chunky's slumping shoulder.

Derek mumbled, "Don't worry about it, man." Derek was the best player on the Bulls, and also the quietest.

But when MJ also went over to Chunky and said, "Hey, it could have happened to anyone—no big deal," Will exploded.

"Yes, it *is* a big deal!" he yelled in exasperation. "Every one of us shoots twenty free throws at every practice.

Chunky can make 'em in practice. But he's got to be able to make 'em at crunch time too."

Will was shaking. He felt everyone staring at him. Nobody said anything, but the glare he got from Nate was especially severe. Will knew Nate hated it when one Bull criticized another.

But Will didn't care what anyone else thought. He was tired of all the wimpy excuse-making. *We blew a game we never should have lost to the sorry Plainview Lions,* he thought bitterly. *And it was all Chunky's fault!*

CHAPTER 3

"All right," Jim said, clapping his hands. "Let's start with Derek and MJ at the forwards, Dave and Mark at the guards, and Chunky at center."

Hey, what's going on here? Will wondered. *Me, not starting?* He felt his face get hot. Since the Bulls had been formed, Will had always been one of the main men.

After some hesitation, the players Jim had named began taking their positions on the blacktop basketball court at Jefferson Park where they always practiced. Nobody seemed quite sure of what was going on.

Will glanced at Brian and Jo, the two other regulars who had not been asked to start. They looked just as confused as he felt.

But only Will spoke up.

"What is this—a joke?" he asked both coaches. "We lose one game to Plainview and three of the starters get *benched?*"

Jim held out his hands in a let-me-explain manner. "We just want to try something new today in practice—and we might try it again next Saturday in the game against Winsted."

Will turned to Brian and Jo and mouthed, "This should be interesting." Then he gave his brother a skeptical look, as if to say, *we're waiting.*

"What we'd like to try," Jim continued, "is to have Brian, Jo, and Will coming in off the bench for a change."

Brian ran his right hand through his short fade haircut and rolled his eyes. "Yeah, that's *obvious*," he said.

"We picked that up already. The question is, *why?*"

"We want to get the guys who are usually the subs into the flow early, so they'll be more ready in case we need them in crunch time," Jim answered readily. *Too readily,* Will thought. Jim's answer sounded rehearsed.

"How come you never felt that way before?" Will asked suspiciously. "In the Plainview game, you didn't put Chunky in until I fouled out. You weren't worried about getting in the subs in *that* game."

"Yeah, and look what happened to us in the Plainview game," Jim retorted. "Maybe I learned something."

"*That* would be a first!" Mark chimed in.

All the Bulls laughed. It was a standing joke that Jim never liked to try anything new, or to admit when he was wrong.

In the midst of the laughter, Nate bent over and palmed a basketball in his huge right hand. Then he took a few loping strides toward the near basket on the blacktop, soared toward the rim, and jammed the ball through the hoop. As he walked back to the group of Bulls, the backboard was still shaking.

Will had seen Nate do this at least a hundred times, but it was still an awesome sight. The tall high-school star usually slammed one down like that to focus the Bulls' attention.

"What we're trying here doesn't only have to do with crunch time," Nate said, picking up where Jim had left off. "Jim and I have also been feeling kind of bad about how little the subs have been playing."

So that's it, Will realized. Divvying up the minutes more fairly had always been one of Nate's themes.

Guess he's finally convinced my brother to go along with it.

"This isn't the NBA, you know," Nate continued. "You guys are in fifth grade, and you're just learning to play hoops. You should all get a decent amount of playing time."

Will looked at his brother questioningly. He knew Jim had never been concerned about spreading the playing time around fairly before.

"Nate's right," Jim said, though Will didn't think he sounded very convincing.

As Dave dribbled the ball with his right hand, he held his left hand high, two fingers up, signaling a set play. Derek, MJ, and Chunky all went into motion. But Mark just stood where he was, slightly to the left of the foul line, looking lost.

From his defensive position, Brian called out, "Earth to Mark. Can we help you?"

Mark hit himself on the head. "Two!" he said brightly. "I know that play!"

"*Duh,*" Brian responded sarcastically.

The new so-called starting lineup had been scrimmaging against the two coaches and the three new "subs" for almost an hour, and Will was not impressed. He looked over at Jim, shaking his head, as if to say, *I told you this wasn't going to work.*

On the starters' next possession, Derek was wide open six feet from the hoop, but MJ's hurried pass was too low and hit him in the feet, bouncing off the blacktop, out of bounds.

As MJ ran to retrieve the ball, Jim called after him. "How many times have I told you to pass to your man's chest, not his sneakers?"

"I know, I know," MJ said, embarrassed.

He does *know,* Will thought. *MJ knows the game better than any of the Bulls out here—besides me. He just can't* play *it very well. And that's why he shouldn't be starting.*

For most of the scrimmage, Will had kept his observations to himself. But when he drove to the hoop against Chunky, and the pudgy center just stepped aside and let him score, Will couldn't contain himself.

"What is this—the *matador* defense? Is *this* what I spent half of last summer teaching you?" Will threw up his hands and looked at Jim and Nate. "I really don't think this is working out very well."

Jim clapped his hands together. "Enough for today," he announced. "It's H-O-R-S-E time."

But as the Bulls began to scramble into a line for their ritual practice-ending game of H-O-R-S-E, Nate called out, "Hold on! I almost forgot. Jim and I got word today before practice that the league all-star teams have been selected."

Will could feel his heart pounding. Everybody knew that the Danville County Basketball League would be selecting an early-season all-star team, based on last season's performances, for a game to be played at the end of the month. He'd been waiting to get the word for weeks.

Nate cleared his throat. "On the East squad," he called out, trying to sound like the public-address announcer at the United Center in Chicago, "representing *your* Branford Bulls, number sixteen, *Derek Roberts!*"

All the Bulls burst into wild applause. Derek just looked down modestly at his sneakers.

"Hey, now *there's* a surprise!" Mark wisecracked. Derek was widely recognized as one of the top players in the league. That he'd make the all-star team was a foregone conclusion.

Will kept listening. *And . . . ?* he thought impatiently. *And . . . ?*

"And also from the Branford Bulls," Nate continued, after a pause that seemed to Will to last forever, "number fourteen, *Will Hopwood!*"

An equally boisterous round of applause followed the announcement of Will's name. Will jumped up, pumped his fist in the air, and shouted, "All right! All right! Who's the man? Who's the *man?*"

"Okay, calm down, guys," Jim said, raising his voice to be heard. "And before anyone feels like they got cheated or dissed, let me explain that the league rule was two players per team. Period."

Jim was looking at Brian, Dave, and Jo as he spoke. Will realized that without the two-players-per-team rule, it was quite possible that all five Bulls starters could have made the squad.

For a moment, Will felt bad for his

teammates who'd been passed over. But then elation from having been picked got the better of him.

He scooted over to Nate with his hand extended for a low five. "Who's the *man?*" he asked one more time, congratulating himself.

Then Will ran to be first in line for the game of H-O-R-S-E. "The guy who shoots after me might as well quit right now," he crowed smugly.

Dave knocked Will's Chicago Bulls cap off his head as the fifth-graders jumped off the bus in front of Benjamin Franklin Middle School.

"Hey, give that back!" Will called, and began to reach for his hat on the sidewalk. But Brian beat him to it, flicking the cap in the air with his toe, then grabbing it before it hit the ground again.

Brian threw the hat to Dave, who snatched it out of the air before Will could lunge for it. Just as Will was about to seriously threaten Dave, he heard the authoritative voice of a teacher rumble, "Settle down, boys. We're not in a playground. This is the school you're entering."

Will wheeled around to see who he and his friends had gotten in trouble with and was relieved to see it was Mr. Neal. The tall science teacher had been Jim's favorite when he was at BFMS, and Will and Mr. Neal had become pretty close as well. Will could see by the look on the teacher's face that he was only kidding with his warning.

"Hey, Mr. Neal, have you heard?" Will asked, loud enough so that anyone within thirty yards could overhear his question. "Me and Derek made the Danville County Basketball League all-star team!"

"That's Derek and I," Mr. Neal corrected, with a big smile on his face. "And congratulations!"

But Will didn't respond. He was too busy checking to see if a certain couple of girls had heard his boast. Standing a few feet away from Mr. Neal were Kristen Albert and Jennifer Suarez. Kristen was generally considered the cutest girl in the fifth grade—and everyone thought of Kristen and Brian as a couple.

But Will happened to think that Jen—with her huge brown eyes and jet-black hair—was every bit as pretty as Kristen. Having her show up at the all-star game so she could see him in action wouldn't be a bad way to impress her. He hoped she'd been listening.

Just to make sure, Will announced to Mr. Neal, in the same loud voice, that the game would be a week from Saturday at the Sampton Community Center.

"We're gonna kick the West's butt," he promised. "You gotta come and see us!"

Dave rolled his eyes for Brian's benefit. "Hey, Too-Tall," the long-haired point guard kidded, using Will's nickname. "I thought you wanted to keep that game a big secret!"

Brian laughed and slapped Dave a low five.

Will realized his friends were making fun of him, but he

didn't care. *They'd be doing the same thing if* they'd *made the team,* he thought.

Later that day in gym class, Mr. Earl, the muscular gym teacher, strode toward the front of the room. Will didn't waste any time. Before Mr. Earl could even call for the kids to line up for calisthenics, Will ran up to him.

"I've got some great news for you, Mr. Earl," he said breathlessly.

Brian and Dave, who were in Mr. Earl's gym class with Will, exchanged knowing looks.

The teacher smiled. "Let me guess," he began. "You're dropping out of school early to enter the NBA draft."

Mr. Earl knew his students. Of course he assumed that if Will had big news, then it must be about hoops.

"You're close," Will answered eagerly. "They picked the Danville County Basketball League all-star team—and guess who made it?"

"Uh, Derek Roberts?" Mr. Earl

answered with a straight face, winking at Brian and Dave. He obviously knew what Will was driving at, but he loved to kid his students. It was one of the reasons he was among the most popular teachers in the school.

"Yeah, Derek Roberts," Will said impatiently. "And Will Hopwood!" Thumping himself proudly on the chest, he added, "You're looking at *the man!*"

"Well, that's great," Mr. Earl said sincerely, extending his hand. "I'm really proud of you."

Will accepted the handshake, and went on to tell the gym teacher when the game would be. "You'll be there, won't you?" Will asked Mr. Earl.

"I'll try," the teacher answered slowly. "But I may have a lot of reading to do that weekend. . . ."

"Mr. Earl!" Will protested. "You can do your reading anytime. This is the biggest—"

"Gotcha!" the gym teacher said with a big grin.

I should have known he was kidding,

Will thought, shaking his head. *He always catches me. I knew Mr. Earl would never miss watching me take everyone to school in the all-star game!*

During the rest of the day, Will also extracted promises to attend the game from Ms. Darling, his English teacher; Mr. Dupont, his social studies teacher; Mr. Charles, his math teacher; and Dr. Byrum, the principal. He must have told at least forty kids about it too.

He waited in front of the school to get on the bus with Brian and Dave. "Okay, are you ready for duty on the second unit at practice this afternoon?" Brian asked as they tromped toward their seats in the middle of the bus.

Second unit? Will thought, puzzled. *Oh yeah, that dumb idea about starting the game on the bench, so some of the subs could get in early.* Since the afternoon before, when Nate and Jim had delivered the news about the all-star team, Will hadn't given the Bulls' problems another thought.

"I forgot about that," Will admitted.

"Yeah, well I didn't," Brian continued. "You know, at first the idea of you and me coming off the bench seemed really lame. But then I got to thinking about it. How would you feel if you were Mark?"

"What do you mean?" Will asked.

"Well, Mark was a starter before Jo joined the team," Brian went on. "Now he never gets to start anymore."

"And don't forget about Chunky and MJ," Dave added. "There are some games they barely get in at all." He shook his long blond hair out of his eyes. "That must not feel too cool."

"Easy for you to say," Will retorted. "You're not one of the starters being benched so they can play."

"Well, I guess certain players are just untouchable," Dave kidded.

Will smirked.

"Seriously," Dave continued. "I'm not saying I *agree* with what Jim and

Nate are doing. I'm just saying I kind of get what they're thinking."

"I get what they're thinking too," Will answered hotly. "It's just that everyone around here is doing too *much* thinking. The bottom line is, we should be trying to win basketball games. Whatever it takes—*whoever* it takes—that's the way we have to go."

Brian and Dave were staring at him. So were a lot of other kids on the bus. Will became aware that his voice had gotten a good bit louder than he'd intended.

Hey, who cares if they all heard me? he thought. *I didn't say anything wrong. I just like to win. Everyone knows that.*

He glared back at each kid individually, until they all stopped looking at him.

CHAPTER 5

"I'm on the Danville County all-star team, but I don't start on the Bulls. Now *that* makes a lot of sense," Will fumed sarcastically to Brian, who was sitting alongside him on the bench.

Brian just shrugged, as if to say, *What can I tell you?*

Will took a swig from his squeeze bottle, then dropped it back down on the floor in disgust. Jim had just announced the Bulls' starting lineup for their game against the Winsted Wildcats. It was the same one they'd been using all week during practice at

Jefferson: Dave and Mark at the guards, Derek and MJ at the forwards, Chunky in the middle.

And Jo, Brian, and Will on the bench.

True, Will had to admit, after that disastrous Monday practice, the scrimmages had gone more and more smoothly as the new first unit got used to working together. *But everyone still knows what the* real *starting lineup should be,* Will thought. *Why are we going with this bogus one?*

Will heard the sound of sneakers screeching on hardwood as the Bulls, in their red jerseys, took the court against the Wildcats, in olive green. The gym in the Winsted Community Center was one of Will's favorites. The floor was always polished and the footing was good—not like the slippery surfaces in some of the other gyms.

As long as the bench is comfortable, I guess that's my only concern today, Will reflected bitterly.

Throughout the first half, and even well into the third quarter, Jim and Nate made substitutions constantly. With twenty minutes of the game gone, everyone's playing time was just about equal.

Man, they're sure not giving anyone a chance to complain today, Will thought, as players were rotated in and out every couple of minutes.

But though the substitution pattern may have been fair, it never allowed the Bulls to get into a rhythm. And it created a lot of confusion.

At one point, the Bulls had six players on the floor. A few minutes later, they had only four.

The constant shuffling resulted in some unusual combinations for the Bulls—some of them not very strategic.

For one stretch late in the first quarter, neither Dave nor Jo was in the game, leaving a shaky Mark at point guard. And midway through the second quarter, both Will and Chunky were on the bench, forcing the Bulls to play several minutes without a legitimate center.

The whole thing made no sense to Will.

With four minutes to go in the third quarter, Jim called a time-out. The Bulls were behind 33–22.

"Guys, you're not boxing out. The

Wildcats are getting too many second shots," Jim complained.

"And you're not moving your feet on defense," Nate chimed in. He did a little dance on the balls of his feet to demonstrate what he meant. "These guys are just blowing right by you."

The Bulls listened mutely.

"Nobody's got anything to say?" Nate asked. "What, are you guys in a state of shock or something?"

Why shouldn't we be? Will thought. *You two have been shuffling us in and out like a deck of cards—and we're down by eleven to the Winsted Wildcats!*

"All right," Jim said, clapping his hands. "We're going to go with Will, Derek, Brian, Dave, and Jo. See if we can't climb back into this game."

It was the first time all afternoon the "real" starting five would be together as a unit. Will glared at his brother.

"Is there a problem?" Jim asked.

"*Now* you put in the starting lineup?" Will replied. "Late in the third quarter, down by eleven?"

Nate answered quickly for Jim. "Hey, look, everyone got a chance to play. Now let's see if we can come back and beat these guys. Come on," he said, putting his hand in the middle of the circle of Bulls. "One, two, three—"

"Show time!" the Bulls responded.

Will just shook his head as he took the floor.

In the next two minutes, Ron Rice, the Winsted center, *twice* got offensive rebounds over Will that he converted into baskets. And Rice was two inches shorter than Will.

"Come on, Too-Tall. Box out!" Nate exhorted. "That guy's taking you to school!"

Will looked coldly at Nate without answering.

Moments later, Gene Walker, Winsted's best all-around player, beat Derek with a spin move, and began driving hard to the basket. Will had position in the paint, between Walker and the hoop. But instead of standing his ground and trying to stop the Wildcats' muscular forward, Will just stepped aside and let him score. *Does it really make any difference now?* he thought.

"What was *that*, Hopwood, the *matador* defense?" he heard Chunky taunt from the bench.

Will gave Chunky a dirty look.

With about a minute left in the quarter, Jason Fox, Winsted's other forward, held the ball in the left corner. Brian lashed out and knocked it loose. It rolled toward the Bulls' bench.

Will, the closest Bull, started after the ball. With a dive to the floor, he could have saved it. But Will stayed on his feet. *Why risk a floor burn with the game already down the tubes?* he figured.

The ball rolled out of bounds.

"Green ball," the ref called out.

As Will got ready to play defense, he glanced over at his brother. Jim was seething.

Ticky Brown, the Winsted point guard, inbounded to Rice, who swung the ball around to Fox. Fox squared up and drained a jumper.

Before Dave could bring the ball past mid-court for the Bulls, the buzzer sounded, ending the quarter.

As the Bulls gathered listlessly around the two coaches, Jim hissed, "Nate, you talk to the team." Then he pulled Will down to the far end of the bench for a private conversation.

"How *dare* you not dive for that loose ball?" Jim spat out in a voice he was trying—not very successfully—to keep under control.

Will shrugged. "What difference did it make?" he asked. "We were down by about twelve at the time."

"You little prima donna," his brother replied, his voice rising. "You know, on some team, one of these years, you may not be a star. You may not even be a *starter.* So you better get used to coming off the bench and contributing any way you can."

Will knew he'd be better off not responding. But he couldn't resist.

"Jim," he answered. "It was garbage time."

"Garbage time?" Jim replied. "You call the third quarter *garbage time?* Well, I've got news for you. That's when Mark and Chunky and MJ usually get in—and *they* don't think it's garbage time. *They* manage to give it their all.

And that's what I expect out of *you!*"

Will stared down at his sneakers. He didn't dare answer his brother back again, but he refused to look him in the eye.

Not wanting to get in any further trouble, Will hustled just enough in the fourth quarter.

The Bulls' regulars played most of the period and cut into Winsted's big lead—but not enough to make a serious run for the game.

The Wildcats won, 50–43.

"Hey, everyone contributed today," Nate said as the players tromped toward the Bowman's Market van, known as the Bullsmobile. "You guys should feel real good about that."

"And we made things interesting at the end," Jim added. "I'll bet we scared Winsted a little bit."

Will hated it when the coaches forced this happy chatter. He didn't feel real good about anything, and the sour expression on his face showed it.

"What's the problem now, Too-Tall?" Nate asked.

Will shook his head from side to side and then stopped to stare at Nate and Jim. "I just want to know what you guys are trying to prove," he answered. "Now we've managed to lose to Plainview *and* Winsted. Will you be satisfied when we lose to every sorry team in this league?"

Jim gave Will a sharp, threatening look—but this time Will stared right back.

None of the other Bulls said anything. Their silence made Will even more certain that he was right.

CHAPTER 6

Mark looked down at his feet, then took a step backward so he was outside the three-point circle. Lowering the ball to his hip, he hoisted up his trademark shot-put-like heave.

"Another long-range bomb," Mark announced, raising his two hands high. "Just like those two guided missiles I launched against the Wildcats yesterday!"

Mark pulled off his

prescription goggles and wiped them clean with his T-shirt—something it seemed to Will  that Mark did about twenty times an hour, whether he needed to or not.

"Yeah, you just keep shooting from downtown like that," Chunky challenged. He had himself planted in the paint, under the basket. "Take all the threes you want, but you try to bring something in here, and I'll send it right back, just like I did against Ron Rice yesterday in the third quarter."

Will listened to the friendly trash talk between Chunky and Mark. There was one thing he couldn't deny: The subs certainly seemed upbeat over their playing time and what they'd accomplished yesterday—even though the Bulls *had* lost to Winsted.

The Sunday shoot-around took place at the blacktop court in Jefferson Park, an open space in the middle of Branford full of trees, a lake, and a playground.

The shoot-around was a loose, players-only activity. Jim and Nate never showed up. But the coaches had made it clear that although attendance wasn't required, it was a good idea for the players to be there—*especially* on Sundays following a Bulls' loss.

Chunky, Mark, and MJ were horsing around at the end of the blacktop nearest the lake. The five regular starters were clustered at the opposite hoop, watching the subs go at it.

"Hey, I think it's great that those guys finally feel they've *done* something," Jo said, adjusting the green baseball cap she always wore backward. "So what if we lose a game once in a while?"

Jo had good reason to know what it felt like to be an outsider, Will realized. The summer before, when she'd tried out for the Bulls, a lot of the guys didn't want her on the team because she was a girl. And for some time in the fall, her teammates froze her out because they thought she was being a ball hog.

"Yeah," Derek agreed. "When MJ went coast to coast and scored on that fast break in the second quarter yesterday, it must have been his highlight of the season!"

Derek's enthusiastic response took Will by surprise. The Bulls' spaghetti-thin forward was almost as well known for his silence as he was for his basketball heroics.

"But I think Jim had brain lock by not putting us in until halfway through the third quarter," Dave said, tugging his shorts down even lower so they hung well below his knees. By "us," he had meant the five regulars clustered around the hoop.

"Oh, come on, Droopy," Brian said, using Dave's nickname. "We still had plenty of time to catch up. We just didn't get it together."

Will listened to the back-and-forth chatter of his teammates and wondered why he was the only one who seemed to get the main point.

"Anybody here notice that we're

oh-and-two?" he asked, sounding ir-
ritated. "Did you know the Bulls
have *never* lost two in a row before?
But maybe that's okay, as long as it
puts a smile on MJ's face—"

"Speaking of faces," Dave interrupted,
"here come a bunch of real ugly ones."

Will, Brian, Derek, and Jo all
looked up and saw three kids saunter-
ing down the narrow paved path to
the blacktop. One of them had a crew
cut and his pudgy face was twisted in
a nasty expression. Another was a
tall, lanky kid wearing a black wool
cap. The third was short and skinny,
and had a mop of bright red hair.

Will recognized them immediately as
Otto Meyerson, Jo's obnoxious brother,
and his Sampton sidekicks, Spider and
Matt. The Sampton Slashers were always right up there with the Bulls as
the top two teams in the league, but
they were the most annoying group of
wiseguys Will had ever met.

"Well if it isn't the three stooges,"
Brian said with a sneer.

"Well, if it isn't the pathetic, last-place Bulls," Spider shot right back.

Will usually tried to ignore *everything* the Slashers said, but Spider's remark hit home. He angrily tried to think of a stinging reply, but he was tongue-tied.

"What are you jerks doing here?" Jo asked. "This is Branford Bulls territory."

"Oh, *excuse* me," Matt said with mock politeness. "I forgot you guys call this dump of a court your home." The Slashers always poked fun at the Bulls for being the only team in the league without an indoor court, and for having to hold their practices outdoors at Jefferson.

Otto grabbed the ball from Jo's hand and carelessly put up a long shot with barely a look at the basket. It went in.

"I just came to tell my wittle sister that Mom wants her home by five," he said.

Will knew that was a total lie. Otto and his buddies had come over for one reason only: to taunt the Bulls about being beaten by the Wildcats. They never missed a chance to show up after a Bulls' defeat.

"Why don't you guys crawl back into your hole?" Will said in disgust. "We're in the middle of a practice. And *some* of us—" with a sweep of his arm he indicated Derek and himself—"have an all-star game to get ready for."

Otto came over and put a hand on Will's shoulder. "This is truly touching," he said, his voice oozing with sarcasm. "You guys are on the all-star team too. We'll be *teammates!*"

Will shoved Otto's hand off his shoulder. *Teammates!* he thought with horror. He'd never even considered the possibility that Otto would be on the all-star team too. But Jim had told them that two players from each team were being selected. *Of course* Otto would be one of the Slashers.

Enjoying Will's surprise and discomfort, Otto went on. "Spider here made the team too. You and me and Spider and Derek—all part of one big, happy family! Haven't you seen the roster?" Otto reached into the back pocket of his oversized jeans and pulled out a crumpled-up piece of paper. As he dramatically unfolded it, all five Bulls gathered around and eyed it anxiously:

DANVILLE COUNTY BASKETBALL LEAGUE
ALL-STAR ROSTER

EAST SQUAD	WEST SQUAD
Elvis Bailey—Harrison	Air Ball Archibald—Portsmouth
Jason Fox—Winsted	Sky Jones—Essex
Devon Haskins—Harrison	Kyle Liu—Torrington
Will Hopwood—Branford	Wilder MacCrae—Clifton
Spider McHale—Sampton	Spuds Marinaro—Rochester
Terrell Means—Plainview	Sean McClain—Essex
Otto Meyerson—Sampton	Bulldog O'Neil—Clifton
Derek Roberts—Branford	Madison Orantes—Torrington
Gene Walker—Winsted	Rowdy Rollins—Rochester
Moose Williams—Plainview	Bucky Skrensky—Portsmouth
Coach: Mike Peroni, Harrison	Walt Kowalsky, Portsmouth

Will, still in shock over having to share his moment of glory with the likes of Otto Meyerson and Spider McHale, felt the need to say something. "Well," he boasted, "you guys may be on the team—but I'm gonna be *the man!*"

"Are you kidding?" Otto retorted. "You'll be *the man?* You won't even be a *starter.*"

Will narrowed his eyes. "Yeah, and just how do you happen to know that?" he asked, trying not to sound too alarmed.

Otto gave Will a look as if he, Otto, was the teacher and Will was a painfully slow student.

"Did you get a good look at the roster, genius?" he asked Will. "At the bottom, where it says 'Coach'?" Otto jabbed at the sheet of paper with his index finger. "Mr. Peroni, the Hornets' coach, is running the team. Elvis Bailey of the Hornets is on the team. Now *you* tell *me* who's going to be the starting center."

Will's mind clicked back over recent games between the Bulls and the Hornets. He knew he could eat Bailey, the Hornets' center, for lunch. But he'd once had a big run-in with Elvis Bailey and Bailey's cousin, a bully named Travis Barnes. The ordeal resulted in some very hard feelings between Will and the Hornets.

Could Otto be right? Will wondered miserably. *Could Elvis Bailey start at center over me? I wouldn't put it past Mr. Peroni. . . .*

Will felt a funny sensation in his stomach as he thought about how many people he'd told to go to the all-star game over the past few days. He began to wonder if that had been such a good idea after all.

I can't believe this! Will said to himself, scanning the bleachers in the Sampton Community Center gym.

He had never seen the gym this packed before—not even for the Bulls–Slashers championship game last season. He knew the gym at Sampton had been chosen for the all-star game because it was the newest and biggest in the league. The court was NBA-size, the backboards were glass, the floor was perfectly waxed and glistening—and the bleachers could seat about twice as many fans as the gym in Winsted, the next biggest arena available.

And with all that space, there was barely room to squeeze in another body!

Will felt his heart racing. He'd been waiting for this day for weeks! But mixed in with the excitement was a feeling of dread centered in the pit of his stomach. *Could Otto have been right?* Will looked at Elvis Bailey, in his yellow Hornets jersey. *Will Bailey be the starting center instead of me?*

Will glanced up and tried to find the people he knew in the stands. The first sight that caught his eye was a bunch of red jerseys on the top row of the bleachers behind the East squad's bench: The Bulls had come to support their two all-stars. At the end of the same row were Jim and Nate, in their blue-and-white Branford High varsity jackets.

Several rows below, Will spotted his parents. They were sitting with Derek's dad, Harold "Rebound"

Roberts, a former NBA star, and his wife, Beverly. Two sections to the right of his parents was a group of teachers from Benjamin Franklin Middle School—Mr. Neal, Ms. Darling, Mr. Earl, Mr. Dupont, Mr. Charles, and Dr. Byrum among them.

And way up high above the teachers he caught sight of Kristen Albert and Jennifer Suarez. So they had come! Actually, he realized, pretty much everyone he'd asked had shown up—not to mention all the other kids he recognized from BFMS and from the various teams around the league.

Will's survey of the stands was interrupted by the nasal voice of Coach Peroni. "All right, let me give you the starting lineup," he said in the nonchalant tone he always used. The coach really rubbed Will the wrong way.

Mr. Peroni had curly brown hair and looked like he had been an athlete, except that now he had a generous potbelly. He didn't smile a lot, and his eyes were always red and puffy. The coach walked in kind of a show-off strut that Will found very annoying.

"We're going to go with Otto Meyerson and Devon Haskins at the guards," Coach Peroni began. He pulled each player up off the bench by the front of his jersey as he called the names.

Figures he starts Haskins, Will thought. *Terrell Means is a better guard—but Haskins is on the Hornets.*

"Derek Roberts and Gene Walker will play the forwards," Coach Peroni continued, yanking the two players to their feet. "And at center—"

Will held his breath.

"Elvis Bailey. Nonstarters, don't worry. There will be plenty of substitutions."

Will felt like he'd been hit in the stomach by a no-look pass. He barely

heard the business about "plenty of substitutions."

What Otto said was true! Will thought, amazed. *That sleazeball really did start his own sorry center over me! Everyone I know in the world is up there watching—and here I am on the bench, twiddling my thumbs.*

Will stared at Coach Peroni with fury. He couldn't believe that the Harrison coach had the nerve to start two Hornets. It wasn't as if the Hornets were one of the league powerhouses!

Coach Peroni probably remembers all too well how I destroyed Elvis Bailey, Will realized. *And I'm sure he remembers the time I ripped that rebound out of Bailey's hands and hit the game-winning basket. I suppose this is his idea of payback.*

Will sat on the bench with his hands covering his face as the game began, but he peeked out just enough to see the East get off to a fast start. After three minutes, the East led 12–4, and Derek Roberts had done the bulk of the scoring.

Each time Coach Peroni looked

down the bench, Will felt a surge of adrenaline. But the first time the coach was looking for Jason Fox. Then Terrell Means. Then Spider McHale.

And still no call for Will Hopwood.

Will looked up and located Jennifer Suarez in the bleachers. She seemed to be half watching the game, half talking with her friends—having a good time.

I'm sure I'm impressing the heck out of her with my bench warming, Will thought bitterly.

Just before halftime, Coach Peroni called out, "Hey, Elvis, take a break!"

Will's heart leaped. *Finally,* he thought thankfully.

But the coach looked right past him.

"Williams!" the coach yelled at the bulky center from Plainview. "Go on in for Bailey."

Will just sat there, stunned.

The second half was more of the same. Otto Meyerson played almost every minute. Elvis Bailey played almost every minute. But Will seemed to be invisible. He was beginning to resign himself to not getting into the game at all.

Again Will stole a glance up at the stands. The teachers he'd invited looked like they were enjoying the game well enough. *They probably don't even realize that I haven't gotten my butt off the bench yet,* Will thought. But things were different with his parents and Nate and Jim. They all looked visibly upset.

As the minutes ticked away in the third quarter, Will's embarrassment gradually turned to seething anger. *Just because I made his team look bad, he takes it out on me personally?* Will thought furiously. *And in front of a packed gym!*

Finally, with 3:30 to go in the game and the East squad up by 51–33, the curly-haired coach

looked down at Will and said, "Okay, Hopwood, you're in for Bailey."

Will felt dull. The edge was off his desire to play. He didn't jump off the bench, but raised himself up slowly. *Me—Will Hopwood—being sent in for garbage time?* he thought with horror.

But as he walked slowly to the scorer's table, his mind turned to all the people who had come to see him play: his mom and dad, his brother and Nate, Brian and Dave and the rest of his Bulls' teammates, his teachers. And Jennifer Suarez.

Will managed to turn his bitterness over being sent in for garbage time into a different kind of resolve. *I have three minutes and thirty seconds*, he said to himself. *I'm going to show everyone here what I can do!*

Will checked in and took a few deep breaths as he jogged to his center position. He felt a little stiff from having sat on the bench the entire game.

When Terrell Means inbounded the ball to Jason Fox, it looked to Will like a blur. *Man, you really lose your rhythm when you're not in the middle of the action,* Will realized, surprised.

Fox worked the ball in to Will in the pivot. Will saw Derek open in the right corner, but he was determined to score himself—determined to make up for lost time. He pump-faked up and down, up and down, but couldn't seem to shake Spuds Marinaro, the center from Rochester who was guarding him.

It was the whistle—and the referee was pointing at Will. "Three seconds, number fourteen," the ref called out.

"Come on, Hopwood!" Coach Peroni called out from the sideline. "*Do* something with the ball. Don't just stand there!"

Will felt his cheeks burn. He looked

up at Jennifer, but couldn't tell if she'd noticed his screwup or not.

On the East squad's next possession, Will again got the ball in the paint. This time he was determined to move more quickly. He jockeyed for position against Marinaro, and was just about to go up for a turnaround jumper when *smack!* The ball was batted out of his hands by Kyle Liu, Torrington's slim, quick forward. It

seemed to Will that Liu had come out of nowhere.

That's great, Will thought. *My second turnover and I haven't been in the game for sixty seconds!*

Before the contest was over, Will had certainly caught everyone's attention—but not exactly in the way he'd had in mind. In trying to play a game's worth in those three-and-a-half short minutes, everything he touched went wrong. All in all, Will had two turnovers, and he was oh-for-three from the field and oh-for-two from the foul line. He didn't grab a single rebound.

The East won, 54–38. As the announcement was being made that Derek Roberts had been named the game's Most Valuable Player, Will wished there was some place he could go and hide. He couldn't even look at his family or his friends.

Will had never felt so humiliated in his life.

Will just wanted to go home and be by himself, but his teammates had other ideas. Even though the all-star game was a once-a-year event, the Bulls did the same thing after the game as they did on any other Saturday: They headed over to Bowman's Market for cold sodas and a rehash of the game.

The bright green-and-white-striped awning of Bowman's was visible from the entrance to Jefferson

Park, but convenience wasn't the only reason that the shop had become the Bulls' headquarters. All the kids loved hanging out with Nathaniel Bowman, Sr., Nate's dad. The balding, roly-poly shopkeeper had been a big-time college player in his day, and was the Bulls' biggest fan. It was Mr. Bowman who had given most of the players their nicknames.

The generous store owner always provided free sodas following Bulls' victories—and he did the same today. "Since the East beat the West, I consider that a win for the Bulls," Mr. Bowman had said when the boys tromped in.

Now he lifted a can of soda, as if making a toast, and said, "Anytime two of my boys play on a countywide all-star team, that's cause for celebration." The Bulls, seated on counter stools, hoisted their cans and clinked them together in response.

Will was not sitting with the rest of the Bulls. Instead, he'd chosen one of the two booths across from the counter. He raised his can of soda halfheartedly. *I hardly feel like an all-star after my performance today!* he thought glumly.

"All right, boys," Mr. Bowman demanded, rubbing his large hands together. "Details. I need details." Mr. Bowman was seldom able to make it to the Bulls' games because he had to mind the store, but he hungrily devoured the play-by-play afterward.

"Mr. B., Derek was something else!" Mark began. "He roasted and toasted that hot dog Sky Jones all afternoon. Man, no wonder he was the game MVP!"

Derek fidgeted with the red-white-and-blue wristbands he always wore. He never felt comfortable hearing about what a great player he was.

"Yeah," Brian added. "And our good friend Otto didn't do squat." He looked over at Jo, Otto's sister. "No offense."

"Hey, don't worry about me," Jo laughed. "I know my brother's a scrub. He had four points, if he was lucky. And all I ever hear about at home is his sixteen-points-a-game scoring average!"

Jo didn't feel bad when any of the Bulls dissed her older brother. She'd never quite forgiven him for not letting her try out for the Sampton Slashers—since the Meyersons *were,* after all, *from* Sampton.

Will felt relieved that all the talk was about Derek and Otto so far. He kind of hoped everyone had forgotten about him.

"And how about our other all-star, Too-Tall, sitting all alone in that booth over there?" Mr. Bowman asked at that moment. "How did our high-scoring, tough-defending rebound machine do today?"

So much for everyone forgetting about me, Will realized regretfully. Mr. Bowman was looking right at him with an expectant smile.

What can I possibly tell him? Will thought desperately.

Fortunately, Nate came to his rescue. "To tell you the truth, Pops, old Too-Tall didn't get a whole lot of PT," the store owner's son said, using the slang for playing time. "Coach Peroni kind of buried him on the bench till the fourth quarter."

"And for the few minutes he got in," Dave was quick to point out, "well, he wasn't exactly a human highlight film."

All the Bulls laughed.

Mr. Bowman gave Dave a disapproving look.

But the fast-talking point guard wouldn't be silenced. "No, really, Mr. B.," Dave rattled on. "Will *does* kind of have it coming to him. All week long he's been telling everyone in the world how he was going to be *the man* at the all-star game." Dave went over and poked his friend in the ribs. "Isn't that right, hotshot?"

Will just fixed Dave with an I'll-get-you-later look.

"Well, you have to admit," Jo said, giving Will a smile, "it *was* pretty funny when the ball squirted out of your hands at the final buzzer. I've never seen you shoot an *air ball* before!"

Again the Bulls burst out in laughter as they recalled the comical sight. But Will didn't find it funny at all.

"Just one of those days, Too-Tall?" Mr. Bowman asked sympathetically.

"Yeah, one of those days, Mr. B.," Will mumbled, his head down.

The talk shifted back to Derek's heroics, Sky Jones's showmanship, and Otto's obnoxiousness. Will, alone in his booth, stayed out of the conversation at the counter.

As the talking and laughing and dissing of opposing players went on, Chunky slid onto the red vinyl-covered bench where Will was sitting. Putting his hand on Will's shoulder, the backup center said, "Don't worry about it. Everyone has an off day."

Will nodded his head in thanks.

Then Chunky added casually, "Hey, it isn't easy coming in cold off the bench at the end of a game, is it?"

Will and Chunky stared at each other. Finally, Will dropped his eyes.

"No," he answered. "It isn't."

"I really want to beat these guys!" Nate told the Bulls as they gathered around the coaches in the pregame huddle. This was their first game since the all-star break—and it just happened to be against the Harrison Hornets.

"I think what Coach Peroni did to Will in the all-star game was pure sleaze," Nate continued, heating up as he went along. "And don't forget, these Hornets are two-and-oh, and starting to think they rule. We've got to show 'em what's up!"

Will shifted from foot to foot as

Nate spoke, anxious to begin. He was hoping desperately to be back in the starting lineup. He was itching to make Coach Peroni pay for his public humiliation. He was dying to get his hands on the ball and school Elvis Bailey—over and over again. Above all, he just needed to get out on the floor and put his horrendous performance in the all-star game behind him as quickly as possible.

Will agreed wholeheartedly with what Nate was saying. *How can the Hornets—a good-but-not-great team—be two-and-oh, when the Bulls are oh-and-two?*

And he also appreciated Nate's comment about Coach Peroni. *Seems to me Coach Peroni—and that wiseguy Elvis Bailey—both have a little payback coming their way!* Will vowed.

"Okay," Jim said. "We're going to start with a lineup a little closer to our regular one today. I may have changed things a little *too* much in that loss to Winsted."

The Bulls tightened their circle

around Jim, waiting to hear who would be in the game. Will held his breath.

"Let's go with Derek and Brian at the forwards, Jo and Mark in the backcourt," Jim announced. "Will, you start at center."

Yes! Will cheered silently. He was overjoyed to hear his name in the starting lineup again. He'd show Coach Peroni, Elvis Bailey, and the rest of those losers a thing or two!

But then he saw the crushed expression on Chunky's face. And he heard Chunky's question echoing in his head: *It isn't easy coming in cold off the bench at the end of a game, is it?*

Will thought back to his nightmare experience in the all-star game. *How right he is! And why should it always be Chunky who's shoved into the game late when he's not warmed up and ready? That's not really fair at all.*

Will cleared his throat. "Why don't you give Chunky the start at center?" he suggested to Jim, trying to make it sound as if it were no big deal. "He's been doing fine. And I'm sure I'll get my minutes."

Jim looked at Nate. Nate shrugged.

"Okay," Jim decided. "Then we'll start with Chunky at center."

The game wasn't an easy one for the Bulls. Somehow, against Harrison, it seldom was. They were a pesky squad defensively. Devon Haskins and Drew Schulz, their two guards, had particularly quick hands. And they passed well as a team. Fortunately, their shooting wasn't the best.

The Bulls put together a number of scoring streaks, seeming as though they were going to put the game out of reach. But each time, the Hornets answered with a run of their own, keeping the score close.

After three quarters, the Bulls led 34–32.

The Bulls stood around their coaches, ready for the final period. Jim called for the five players he wanted out on the floor. "Derek and

Brian at the forwards," he said. "Dave and Jo at the guards." Hesitating for a moment, he added, "Chunky, why don't you start the quarter at center."

That's cool—he's trying to even out the minutes, Will realized. He and Chunky had been splitting time at center during the game, and so far Will had gotten a little bit more than his share. And besides, Chunky hadn't done a bad job at all.

Chunky wiped the perspiration off his forehead with the back of his hand. "Put in Hopwood," he said to the coach. Responding to Jim's look of surprise, Chunky added, "I'm really beat."

Will couldn't believe what he was hearing. Chunky was finally getting the playing time he'd craved for so long, he'd performed under pressure, and now he had the opportunity to be in the game when it really counted.

And he was passing it up!

"Are you serious?" Will blurted out.

"Sure, I'm serious," Chunky replied. "I've played a lot more than I'm used to in the last couple of games. And don't forget," he added with a smile, "I carry a little extra weight around." He patted his ample belly.

Will didn't really believe that Chunky was all that tired. Chunky simply knew the Bulls had a better chance of winning with Will in there at center. Chunky just wanted what was best for the team.

Man, Will thought, *Chunky's a pretty neat guy. All he ever really wanted was to play a little part in our wins.*

It was the second time in the game that one player wanted to give up his playing time to another. Jim and Nate looked confused. But again they agreed to the switch.

The Hornets had the ball to start the fourth quarter. Drew Schulz inbounded the ball in the backcourt to Devon Haskins, the Hornets' skinny, left-handed point guard.

As Haskins brought the ball up the floor, Will jockeyed for position in the paint with Elvis Bailey. Bailey was tall and had braces, and he always used his elbows a little more than was necessary. Will had never thought much of his game—or his personality.

And now, after Bailey had gotten the lion's share of the playing time in the all-star game—the share that Will felt should have belonged to him—Will was especially determined to make him look bad.

With the ref looking the other way, Bailey gave Will a shove, trying to clear some space for himself. It worked for a moment, but Will sprung right back to his defensive position, body to body with the Hornets' center.

"Whoa, playing the tight D, huh, Hopwood? I'm impressed," Bailey taunted. "I wasn't sure you knew how to play at all anymore, after the way you looked in the all-star game."

Will didn't answer. He just kept within a breath of his opponent, with his hands in the air. Out of the corner of his eye, Will caught a glimpse of Travis Barnes, Bailey's cousin, in the bleachers. The sight of Barnes made him even more determined to take Bailey to school.

Haskins worked a bounce pass into Bailey, who had his back to the basket. Elvis faked a drive to his left, then wheeled to his right and went up for a jump shot. Will jumped a split second later.

Thwack!

Will swatted the ball forcefully off to the sideline, in the  direction of the Bulls' bench. He was pleased to see the stunned look on Bailey's face.

"Rejection!" Nate screamed, dancing up and down. "I *love* this game!"

Jo hustled to grab the ball just before it went out of bounds, and flung it over her head back into play. Luckily, Dave was in the right place at the right time to make the catch, and he dribbled the ball upcourt for the Bulls.

Dave fired a hard chest pass to Brian, who was open in the left corner—his favorite spot. His shot bounced a few times on the rim, then fell out.

But Will was right there for the rebound. With no wasted time, he made the easy put-back from the right side.

"Where were you, Bailey?" Will heard Coach Peroni screaming from the Harrison sideline. "You're supposed to be boxing Hopwood out!"

Haskins brought the ball up the floor quickly for the Hornets, and again was able to get it into the hands of Elvis Bailey. Bailey didn't appear to be that eager to shoot again, after Will's resounding block. But as he looked around for someone to pass to, Will reached out and took a swipe at the ball, knocking it free.

Dave pounced on the ball and sped upcourt for an unchallenged layup.

Bailey still stood where Will had stripped the ball from him. "He hacked me!" the embarrassed Hornets' center complained to the ref.

"Sorry, son, all ball," Will heard the ref reply. Will flashed Elvis a quick, toothy smile.

Following a miss by Mike Van Siclen, the Hornets' tall, stringy forward, Derek snared the rebound and handed the ball off to Dave. Dave dribbled to the frontcourt, and the Bulls swung the ball around briskly— to Jo, then to Brian, then to Will.

Will held the ball with two hands in front of his belly button, facing the basket. He challenged Elvis with a stare.

A second later, Will pump-faked, to get Elvis off balance, then fell back for his trademark soft turnaround jumper.

"Butter!" a delighted Nate called out from the Bulls' sideline. The excited coach had shot up from his seat and was now jumping up and down.

In less than two minutes, the Bulls, led by Will, had stretched their lead to 40–32 and were turning what had been a tight game into a blowout. But Will was far from finished.

In that fourth quarter alone, Will wound up with eight points, five rebounds, three blocks, and two steals. Most of the damage was done at the expense of Elvis Bailey.

The Bulls won 50–37, pulling farther and farther away as the final quarter wound down. It was the Bulls' first victory and the

Hornets' first defeat of the new season.

"Serves that lowlife Peroni right!" Mark chirped as the Bulls celebrated around their bench.

"And sweet revenge for Will!" MJ added. "I loved watching that so-called all-star Elvis Bailey eat leather three times!" MJ was referring to Will's three monstrous blocks.

"That's right," Nate said, grinning from ear to ear and clapping Will repeatedly on the back. "Too-Tall played like a man on a mission today." Smiling at Chunky, the coach continued, "No offense, but after that performance today, we might need to let Too-Tall have his starting job back."

Will looked at Chunky and winked. "Hey, it's not who starts and who doesn't that matters," Will said. "It's that everyone's pitched in by the end!"

Don't miss Super Hoops #15,
Rebound! Coming soon!

"I thought this was one of the days you were supposed to be at *our* practice," Will said to Jo. "The coaches were counting on you."

Jo didn't like the way Will and Brian were looking at her. She spun her basketball on her right index finger, trying to strike a casual pose.

"Rehearsal for *Annie Get Your Gun* ran late," she said. Seeing that Will was expecting more of an answer, she added, "I couldn't leave in the middle of a scene."

Brian stood straddled over the crossbar of his bike. "If rehearsals run so late all the time," he challenged, "why don't you skip them once in a while?"

"Are you *kidding?*" Jo screeched. "I can't do that! I'd be kicked out of the play!"

Brian just stared back at her, a nasty smile creeping across his face. Jo knew just what he was thinking: *Miss enough practices, and you could be kicked right off the Bulls too!*

About the Author

Hank Herman is a writer and newspaper columnist who lives in Connecticut with his wife, Carol, and their three sons, Matt, Greg, and Robby.

His column, "The Home Team," appears in the *Westport News*. It's about kids, sports, and life in the suburbs.

Although Mr. Herman was formerly the editor in chief of *Health* magazine, he now writes mostly about sports. At one time, he was a tennis teacher, and he has also run the New York City Marathon. He coaches kids' basketball every winter and Little League baseball every spring.

He runs, bicycles, skis, kayaks, and plays tennis and basketball on a regular basis. Mr. Herman admits that he probably spends about as much time playing, coaching, and following sports as he does writing.

Of all sports, basketball is his favorite.